What Can My Ear Hear?

A BOOK ABOUT THE HUMAN BODY

By D. K. Sullivan

Illustrated by Joe Ewers

Consultant: Lindsay Tan, M.D.

A Muppet Press/Golden Book

Hi-ho! Kermit the Frog here with Robin and our pal Abby. Have you ever wondered how your body works? Well, come with us and you'll find out!

What is my body made of?

Your body is an amazing machine. It has skin, bones, blood, muscles, hair, fingernails, ears, eyes, stomach, heart, brain, and much more. All the parts of your body work together to make—you!

How does my body know what to do?

Your brain is the "boss" of your body. It knows what's going on because tiny "wires" called nerves run all over your body. Most of these nerves carry messages to and from different parts of your brain.

What tells your feet to jump and skip? Your brain. What tells you how to blow a bubble? Your brain. What tells you when your stomach hurts? It's your brain!

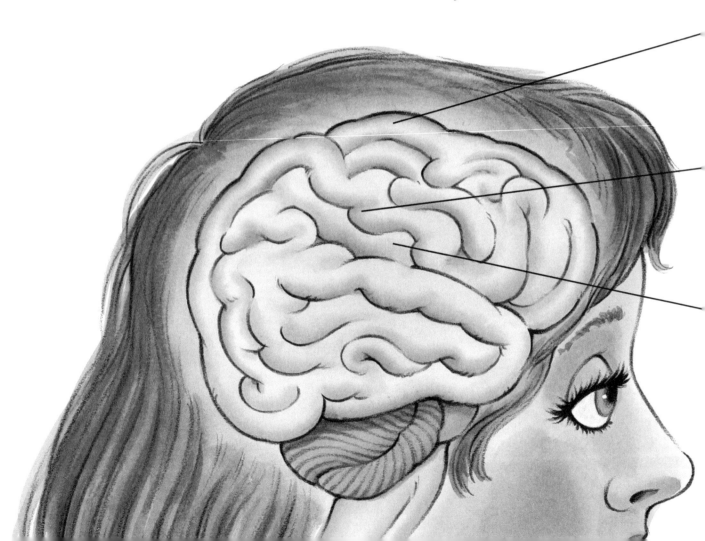

Why doesn't it hurt when I get a haircut?

Your hair doesn't have any nerves at all! Neither do your toenails and fingernails. They can't send messages to your brain that say, "OUCH!"

Why do I have bones?

Your bones give your body its shape. Without bones, you would just be a floppy bag of skin. Bones also protect the inside parts of your body, like your brain, your heart, and your lungs.

Touch your elbow, your knee, your ankle—you're feeling bones!

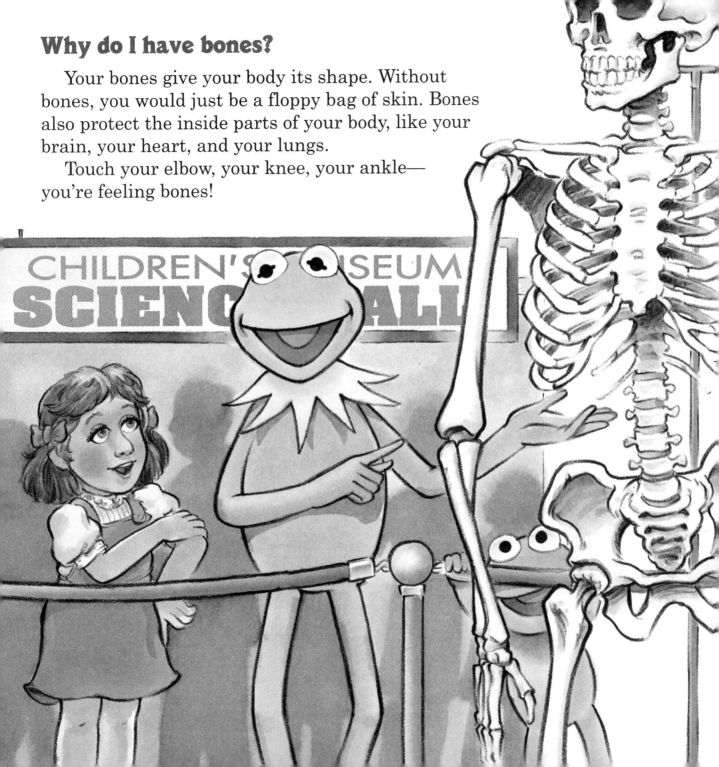

What do muscles do?

Muscles move your body. Some muscles, like the ones in your arms and legs, are connected to your bones. They help you run, skip, or throw a ball. You have muscles everywhere—in your neck, your feet, your fingers, even your nose!

What's the biggest part of my body?

The answer is all over you. Touch your arm. Touch your back. Touch your chin. Your whole body is covered with skin—except your eyes! It is like a waterproof coat that protects you from germs. And just imagine— without skin, all your insides would fall out!

Why do I sweat?

Sweating is how your skin helps you keep cool.
When you are hot, sweat comes out through very tiny
holes on your skin called pores. As the air around you
dries the sweat, you cool off. Sweat is made up mostly
of water with some salt.

What are the black circles in the middle of my eyes?

These circles are called pupils. They let light into your eyes so you can see. When you are in a place that's bright, your pupils get very tiny. When you are in a dark place, they get really big to let in more light.

What can my ear hear?

Lots of things—like music, people talking and singing, and a cat meowing! Inside your ear is a thin piece of skin called an eardrum. Air carries sounds to the eardrum. The vibration of the eardrum is carried as a message to your brain. Your brain then tells you what you're hearing.

How does my nose smell a rose?

When you sniff a rose, air carries the flower's scent
into your nose. From your nose, news of this smell
travels to your brain. Your brain tells you what you're
smelling.

Aaah-choo! What makes me sneeze?

Inside your nose are tiny hairs that catch any dust or dirt you may breathe in. When something tickly gets inside your nose, you automatically sneeze. Your nose is trying to get rid of the tickly thing with a blast of air!

Here's a neat fact: You can't sneeze with your eyes open! Watch what happens the next time you sneeze.

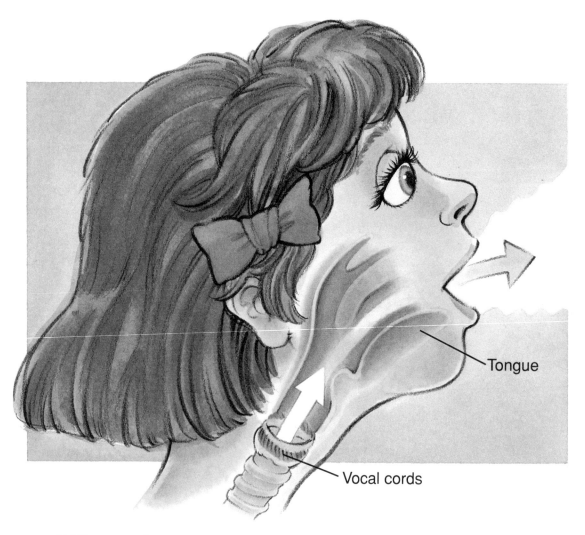

Tongue

Vocal cords

Where does my voice come from?

Inside your throat, right below your tongue, are stringy things called vocal cords. When you speak or sing, air from your lungs pushes against these cords and makes them vibrate. The vibrating air comes out of your mouth as your voice!

How do I taste things?

Stick your tongue out in front of a mirror. Do you see all the little bumps on it? They are taste buds, which help you taste things. You taste most bitter things on the back of your tongue and salty things near the front. The tip of your tongue tastes sweet things. And the sides taste sour things.

Where does my food go after I eat it?

After you chew and swallow your food, it goes down a long tube into your stomach. There the pieces get even smaller. After a while, they become watery and mushy, like baby food.

The food goes out of your stomach, a little at a time, into long, curled-up tubes called intestines.

The intestines sort out the nutrients—which your body needs—from what it doesn't need. From the intestines, the nutrients are absorbed into the blood and carried all over your body.

The part of the food that isn't needed comes out when you go to the bathroom.

Stomach

Intestines

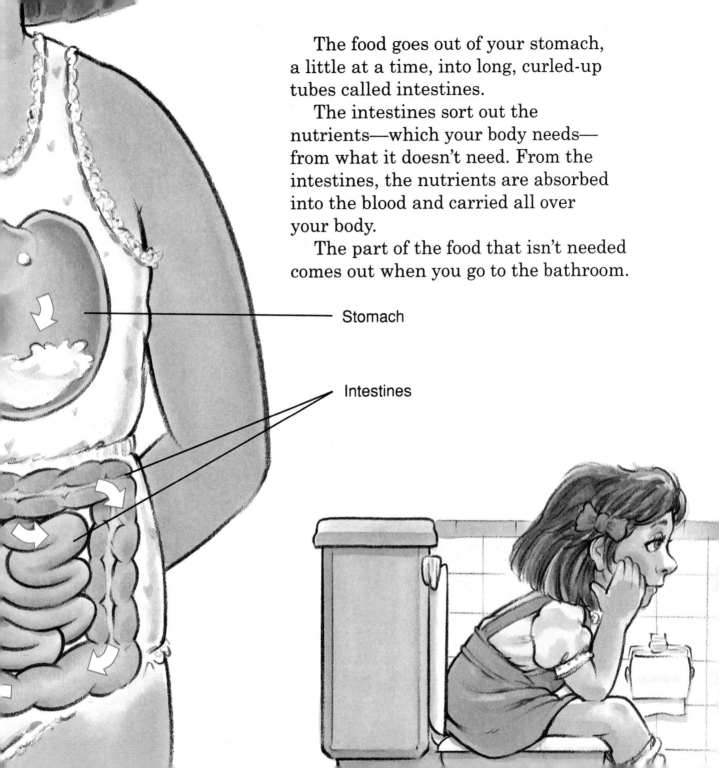

What happens to the air I breathe in?

The air you breathe in through your nose travels down your windpipe. It fills two balloonlike bags in your chest called lungs. Air has oxygen in it, and you need oxygen to live. Oxygen from the lungs goes into your blood, which carries it all over your body.

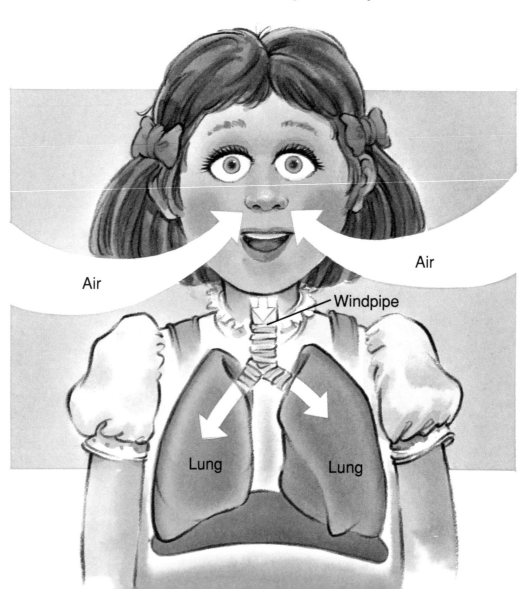

Air

Air

Windpipe

Lung

Lung

Why do I get out of breath sometimes?

Your body works hard when you run fast or play for a while. And that's when you begin to feel out of breath. Your body is saying, "I need more oxygen!"

What does my heart do?

Your heart works like a pump to send blood throughout your body. Blood carries oxygen and nutrients from your head to your toes!

If you listen to your heart, you might hear this: *lub-dub, lub-dub.* That's the sound of your heart beating!

Why do I need to sleep?

Your body works so hard all day, it needs to take a break sometime! When you sleep, your muscles rest and your mind rests. If you don't get enough sleep, you may feel cranky when you wake up!

Your turn!

Did you know your tongue can't taste anything if it's completely dry? Try this easy test:

First, dry your tongue by wiping it with a towel or tissue. Your tongue has to be very, very dry. Then lick some sugar. Can you taste it? What does it feel like?

Wet your tongue again and try tasting the sugar. Now it tastes sweet!